TEENY WITCH

and the Tricky Easter Bunny

by LIZ MATTHEWS
illustrated by CAROLYN LOH

Troll Associates

"Coloring Easter eggs is fun!" cried Teeny Witch.
Splash! Teeny dipped an egg in a cup of coloring.
The egg went in white. It came out a pretty blue color.
"The blue eggs are my favorite."

"I like green," said Aunt Icky.
"I think green eggs are pretty.
All eggs should be green."

"I like purple eggs," said Aunt Ticky.
Aunt Vicky was using a brush, too.
"Which one is your favorite?" Teeny asked
Aunt Vicky.

Aunt Vicky smiled and held up an egg. She had painted red dots with tiny legs. It made the red dots look like tiny bugs.

"I like this one," said Aunt Vicky. "It reminds me of my ugly bug collection."

Ick! thought Teeny. What an awful looking Easter egg! I hope Aunt Vicky doesn't paint any more eggs.

"I can't wait for Easter to come," said Teeny as she dipped another egg. Splash! "I like to hunt for Easter eggs. I like chocolate rabbits and jelly beans. I like the Easter Bunny, too."

"Easter is coming soon," said Aunt Icky. She put
a colored egg into an Easter basket on the table.
"Tomorrow Easter will be here."

"The Easter Bunny may be here before then," said
Aunt Ticky. "Sometimes that tricky rabbit goes out the
day before Easter. He goes out to make sure all the
children are being good."

Aunt Vicky looked at Teeny Witch. "If you are lucky, you may see the Easter Bunny," said Aunt Vicky. "If you are *very* lucky you might even catch him."

Teeny Witch laughed. "Why would I want to catch the Easter Bunny?" she asked.

"Rabbits are lucky," said Aunt Vicky. "The Easter Bunny is the luckiest rabbit of all. His good luck can work magic."

Teeny Witch put a bright red egg in the basket on the table. "Magic?" she said.

Aunt Vicky nodded. "If you catch the Easter Bunny, he will grant you one magic wish."

Aunt Ticky also nodded. "And you can wish for anything you want."

Wow! thought Teeny Witch. If I am lucky, I will catch that big, tricky rabbit. Teeny Witch went out to hunt for the Easter Bunny.

Teeny Witch went to the park. She looked in the bushes. She looked behind trees. She didn't see that big Easter Bunny.

Teeny looked here. She looked there.
She hunted everywhere. The Easter
Bunny was nowhere to be seen.
"Where can that tricky, magic
rabbit be?" asked the little witch.

Just then, Teeny Witch saw something
in a bush on the other side of the park.
Teeny saw two big rabbit ears sticking
out of the bush.

"It's the Easter Bunny!" Teeny cried.

Off she ran toward the bush as fast as she could. "I'll catch that magic rabbit," Teeny said.

The rabbit ears moved. Out of the bush hopped a big white rabbit. The rabbit was as big as Teeny.

"That big rabbit cannot hop fast enough to get away from me," said Teeny.

But the big white rabbit did not hop. It got on a red bike. ZOOM! The bunny rode away fast on the bike.

"What a tricky rabbit!" Teeny shouted as she chased after the bunny.

19

Teeny ran and ran. The big white rabbit rode faster and faster. But the red bike was too fast. Teeny Witch could not catch the rabbit. The rabbit rode away.

"I will not get my wish now," said Teeny sadly. She sat down at a table in the park. "I will never see that rabbit again," she said.

Just then, Teeny did see the rabbit. It was the same white rabbit with big floppy ears. But it was not riding a bike. Now it was on roller skates.

Teeny Witch hopped up. "Come back here, you tricky rabbit!" Teeny shouted. "I want my Easter wish."

The rabbit did not come to Teeny. Zippity-Zoom! Away it skated.

Teeny Witch ran after the rabbit. The bunny skated fast. "I wish I had my bike," said Teeny as she chased the rabbit. "A bike is faster than roller skates."

Zippity-Zoom! The big white rabbit skated away.
"That lucky bunny really is magic," said Teeny.
"It got away from me on a bike. Now it got away
on roller skates. What next?"

A green car went by. Teeny Witch looked at the car. In the back seat of the car she saw two big ears. "It's the Easter Bunny!" said Teeny.

ZOOM! The green car went by fast. There was no way Teeny could catch it. "There goes that tricky rabbit again," said Teeny. "What is going on? Is that rabbit playing a game with me?"

ZIP! A big white rabbit went zooming by on a blue skateboard. "I will catch you now," Teeny Witch called. "A skateboard cannot go very fast."

Teeny Witch ran after the tricky rabbit. She ran very fast. Teeny got closer and closer to the rabbit on the skateboard. "Soon I will catch you," she said.

Just then, the rabbit stopped in front of a school.
It picked up the blue skateboard and walked into the
school yard.

Teeny Witch stopped, too. "Why did that rabbit stop
at that school?" asked Teeny. "Is this a trick?
Is it a game?"

Teeny saw the green car. She saw the red bike.
She saw some roller skates, too.
"What is going on?" said Teeny Witch.

Teeny Witch looked in the school yard. The school yard was full of big white rabbits with floppy ears.

White rabbits were hopping around. Big bunnies were playing games. There were Easter bunnies everywhere!

"Is this magic?" said Teeny.

"It is not magic," someone said. "This is for the school Easter play."

Teeny turned around. She saw a boy in a rabbit suit. He looked just like a real rabbit.

Teeny looked at the other rabbits in the school yard.
They were all boys and girls wearing rabbit suits!
Teeny laughed. She had chased boys and girls in rabbit
suits. She had not seen the real Easter Bunny after all.

"Do you want to stay for our Easter play?" the boy in the rabbit suit asked Teeny.

Teeny shook her head. "Thank you," she said, "but it's getting late. I have to go home now."

Teeny laughed at herself all the way home. "What a funny way to spend the day before Easter," she said.

Teeny went into her house. She went into the kitchen. Her three aunts were at the table.

"Did you see the Easter Bunny?" asked Aunt Icky.

"Did you catch him?" asked Aunt Ticky.

"Did you get a magic wish?" asked Aunt Vicky.

"No," said Teeny Witch. "But I had lots of fun chasing boys and girls in rabbit suits. Tomorrow I will have even more fun."

The next day was Easter. And Teeny Witch did have lots of fun. Her aunts had fun, too. They all hunted for eggs.

They all got big Easter baskets filled
with chocolate rabbits and jelly beans.

"I like Easter," said Teeny Witch. "I did not catch the Easter Bunny. But my magic wish was granted anyway."

"What was your wish?" her aunts asked.

45

"I wished everyone would have a great Easter,"
said Teeny Witch. "And we all did!"